for Klaus

This paperback edition first published in 2007 by Andersen Press Ltd.
First published in Great Britain in 2005 by Andersen Press Ltd., 20 Vauxhall Bridge Road, London SW1V 2SA.
Published in Australia by Random House Australia Pty., Level 3, 100 Pacific Highway, North Sydney, NSW 2060.
All rights reserved.
Copyright © Ruth Brown, 2005
The rights of Ruth Brown to be identified as the author and illustrator of this work have been asserted
by her in accordance with the Copyright, Designs and Patents Act, 1988.
Colour separated by Photolitho AG, Zürich, Switzerland. Printed and bound in Italy by Grafiche AZ, Verona.

10   9   8   7   6   5   4   3   2

British Library Cataloguing in Publication Data available.

ISBN 978 1 84270 475 2

This book has been printed on acid-free paper.

NIGHT-TIME

TALE

Ruth Brown

Andersen Press · London

"Are you awake, Mama? I had a bad dream.
It frightened me so, I can't sleep, Mama.

I was in a dark forest and there was a house . . .

. . . a house made of candy and gingerbread.

I tasted a piece — but an old witch jumped out.
She frightened me so I just ran, Mama.

I ran very fast and bumped into a girl,
a girl who was going to her grandma's.

We went to the house where her gran was in bed.

She smiled at us both, but her teeth were SO big . . .

. . . and her hands and her face were hairy and grey.
She frightened me so I just ran, Mama.

I ran and I ran, then I stopped and looked up —
I saw a great beanstalk that reached to the sky.

A giant slid down and crashed to the ground.
He left a huge hole where he landed.

I went to the edge to see where he'd gone
and felt somebody **PUSH** me, right over.

I fell down and down then woke with a bump.
Can I come in with you? I can't sleep, Mama."

"There, there," Mama said, "there's no need to fear.
They're just fairy tales, they can't hurt you . . .

Come in with me and go back to sleep —
You'll be tired as can be in the morning."

So Baby Bear climbed into Mama Bear's bed . . .

. . . and soon they were peacefully sleeping.